STORYTELLER'S NOTE

In the southern part of Italy, on the Adriatic Sea, is the town
of Barletta. This Adriatic town is quiet; it is not visited
by many tourists. But there is something special in Barletta,
standing right there in front of San Sepolcro Church.
The something special is a gigantic statue of a young man.
Some say it's the largest statue in all of Europe. No one knows
exactly how it got there or exactly who it is supposed
to be. One thing is sure—the people of Barletta love their
Mysterious Giant. They tell stories about him. One of their
favorite stories about the Mysterious Giant is how, in the
eleventh century, the giant statue saved the town of Barletta.

This is that story.

THE MYSTERIOUS GIANT OF BARLETTA

An Italian folktale adapted and illustrated by

TOMIE dePAOLA

HARCOURT BRACE & COMPANY
San Diego   New York   London

Copyright © 1984 by Tomie dePaola

Requests for permission to make copies
of any part of the work should be mailed to:
Permissions Department,
Harcourt Brace & Company, 6277 Sea Harbor Drive,
Orlando, Florida 32887-6777.

Library of Congress Cataloging-in-Publication Data
dePaola, Tomie.
The mysterious giant of Barletta.
Summary: The giant statue that has always stood
in front of the Church of San Sepolcro in Barletta
is called upon to save the town from an army of a
thousand men that is destroying all the towns
and cities along the lower Adriatic coast.
[1. Statues—Fiction.   2. Giants—Fiction]
I. Title
PZ7.D439Gh   1984   [E]   83-18445
ISBN 0-15-256347-4
ISBN 0-15-256349-0 (pbk.)

Reprinted by arrangement with Harcourt Brace & Company.
10   9   8   7   6   5   4   3   2   1

Printed in the United States of America

The paintings were done in waterproof colored inks and
tempera on 140 lb. Fabriano handmade watercolor paper.
The text is Goudy Bold, set by Hillcrest Graphics.
The hand-lettered display type is by Karen Savary.
Separations were made by Heinz Weber, Inc.
Designed by Karen Savary

In the town of Barletta,
in front of the Church of San Sepolcro,
stood a huge statue.
No one knew where it had come from or when.
The Mysterious Giant—
for that is what the people called the statue—
had always been there
as long as anyone could remember.

Even Zia Concetta.
Zia Concetta was the oldest one
in all of Barletta.
She lived right across the square
from the giant statue.
"Every day, every night, for my whole lifetime,
I've looked out the window and there he is,"
she would say.

Good weather and bad,
the Mysterious Giant stood there.
The people of Barletta
loved having the statue
in their town.

In the early morning,
right before the sun came up,
the sisters from the convent
and other townspeople
came to the church for Holy Mass.
They always greeted the giant
with a nod or a smile.

T...
on ...ople
always ...y to market
and aske... the giant
that he giv...
to sell all the...ood luck
or to get a goo...

All day long
the children played around his legs,
and the doves flew around his head.
The young boys would sit
on his big feet
and tell jokes.

A little later
the older boys would sit
on the giant's feet
to watch the older girls walk by.

And at night,
lovers would steal kisses
in the giant's shadow.

Then the streets would be empty.
Doves would settle
on the giant's head and shoulders and arms
and coo themselves to sleep,
and Zia Concetta would open her window and call,
"*Buona notte, Colosso*—good night, Big One."

This was the time the giant loved best.
All was calm, all was still.
Ah, what a peaceful life,
the Mysterious Giant thought.

But one day this peaceful life was over.
Word had reached the town
that an army of a thousand men
was destroying all the towns and cities
along the lower Adriatic coast.
And this army was heading straight for Barletta.
The townspeople ran through the streets in panic.
No one in Barletta was ready
for an army coming to destroy them.
They had no generals, no captains.
Why, they didn't even have any soldiers!

Shouts and screams echoed off the buildings.
The night was lit by torches.
All the peace and quiet was gone.
No doves came to settle
on the Mysterious Giant's shoulders,
and Zia Concetta didn't call "*Buona notte*"
from her window.
The Mysterious Giant didn't like this at all.

The next morning was no better.
It seemed as though everyone
was at the church for Holy Mass,
but there was no market.
No one even smiled,
let alone waved at the Mysterious Giant.
No children played.
Everyone rushed around,
piling their belongings in carts and wagons.
Everyone was getting ready to run from Barletta.
Everyone except Zia Concetta—
and the Mysterious Giant.

"*Colosso*," she said to the huge statue,
"as long as I can remember you have stood here
looking over this town and its people.
Barletta loves you and I know you love Barletta.
I wish you could do something
to save us from this army.
With your size,
I'm sure you could frighten them away.
Why don't you hop down from your pedestal?"

And that's just what the Mysterious Giant did!
"Now . . ." said Zia Concetta.
They put their heads together
and came up with an idea.
"And a good one, too," said Zia Concetta.

The Mysterious Giant climbed back and stood still.
"People of Barletta," Zia Concetta called.
"Come quickly! Great news . . .
un miracolo—a miracle—
our giant is going to save us. Come!"
The people of Barletta gathered around.
"Friends," Zia Concetta said,
"our giant will go to meet this army himself!
All you have to do is three things.
First, bring me the biggest onion you can find.
Second, stay completely out of sight.
Hide under the bed, hide in the closet,
hide in the cellar, hide in the attic,
but stay out of sight.
And third—don't ask any questions!
Have faith in our Mysterious Giant."

Someone quickly brought an onion.
"Now, hide!" shouted Zia Concetta,
and everyone scurried off.
"Well, *Colosso*,"
said Zia Concetta
as she sliced the onion in half,
"buona fortuna."
The Mysterious Giant
took an onion half in each hand,
once more stepped off the pedestal,
and strode off to meet the army.

Three miles outside the city
the Mysterious Giant sat down
by the side of the road
and held the onion pieces close to his eyes.
Big tears began to run down his cheeks.
The giant made loud sobbing noises.

What a sight the army saw as it came over the hill!
"Halt," shouted the captain. The army halted.
"What is that?"
  the captain whispered to one of his lieutenants.
"It looks like a giant boy—crying,"
  answered the lieutenant.
"Well, we'll see about this," said the captain,
  marching off to where the Mysterious Giant sat.

"I am Captain Minckion," the captain declared.
"We have come to destroy this town.
  Who are you, and what are you doing here crying?
  No tricks now—answer me!"
"Oh, sir," said the giant, sobbing,
"I'm sitting out here, away from the town,
  because the other boys in school
  won't let me play with them.
  They say I'm too small.
  They pick on me all the time.
  They call me names,
  like *minuscolo* and *debole*—'tiny' and 'weakling.'
  I'm always the last one chosen for games.
  Today they told me that if I tried to go to school
  they would beat me up.
  I hate being so small."

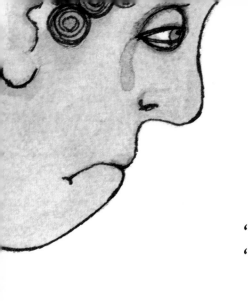

The giant sniffled loudly
and blew the hats off the soldiers standing in front.
The captain and the army stood dumbstruck.
If this giant was a small boy that the others teased,
then imagine what the rest of the people
of this town were like.
"But someday, sir," the giant bellowed,
"someday, I'll show them.
I'm going to eat up all my pasta,
and I'll grow big and strong,
and then I'll be able to fight back."

The soldiers began to back away, trembling.
The lieutenants gathered around the captain,
who had backed away from the giant, too.
There was only one thing to do.
Captain Minckion and his lieutenants
drew their swords.
They held them in the air and shouted. . .

"About-face! Double time—march!"
The army turned and fairly ran
in the opposite direction of Barletta.
The Mysterious Giant threw away the onion halves,
dried his tears,
and went back to the Church of San Sepolcro.

"They're gone,"
shouted Zia Concetta to the townspeople,
as the giant climbed back on his pedestal once more.
"The army is gone. You can come out now.
The town has been saved. Our giant did it!"

Che bella festa!
What a celebration was held that night!

But when it was over
and the moon was high in the sky,
the Mysterious Giant looked out
over the sleeping town.
Doves cooed themselves to sleep
on his head and his shoulders.
Everything was calm, everything was still.
Zia Concetta opened her window.
"Buona notte, Colosso," she called,
"and *grazie.*"